A *Whisper* of War

Gettysburg Ghost Gang # 6

By

Shelley Sykes
and
Lois Szymanski

WHITE MANE KIDS
SHIPPENSBURG, PENNSYLVANIA

For a complete list of available publications
please write
White Mane Kids
Division of White Mane Publishing Company, Inc.
P.O. Box 708
Shippensburg, PA 17257-0708 USA

Library of Congress Cataloging-in-Publication Data

Sykes, Shelley.
    A whisper of war / by Shelley Sykes and Lois Szymanski.
        p. cm. -- (Gettysburg ghost gang ; #6)
        Summary: When the gang's ghost friend, Corporal Jared Scott, tells them about Althea, a woman who fought in the Civil War, Chucky's sister Casey sets out to help this sad ghost find peace.
        ISBN-13: 978-1-57249-327-8 (alk. paper)
        ISBN-10: 1-57249-327-5 (alk. paper)
        [1. Ghosts--Fiction. 2. Soldiers--Fiction. 3. United States--History--Civil War, 1861-1865--Participation, Female. 4. Sex role--Fiction. 5. Gettysburg (Pa.)--Fiction.] I. Szymanski, Lois. II. Title.

PZ7.S9834Wh 2003
[Fic]--dc21

                                                                    2003052517

PRINTED IN THE UNITED STATES OF AMERICA

To the brave Flynn women who have fought their own battles: Katie, the Marine; Stephanie, her mother; and Leslie.

—S.S.

This book is dedicated to the memory of my grandmother, Martha Schmitt, the strongest woman I've known. By example, she taught me how to meet challenges head-on.

—L.S.

Contents

Chapter One

Casey's Wish

Flames from the fire reached out and licked at the fresh pine branches Philip placed on top. They crackled and danced. Chucky, Zach, and Philip settled on logs around the fire, watching the red and white flames as they shriveled the pine needles, turned them brown, and devoured them. Already planted on the log, Casey wiggled her toes closer to the fire, happy to be a part of the boys' circle, for a change.

"Are we going to be on time for Mr. Nesbitt's stories?" Chucky asked Philip.

"Sure!" Zach answered quickly. "I wouldn't miss it."

"I think that is the plan," Philip finally answered.

Philip sensed more than felt the shadow they could not see, and each boy realized at once that they had been joined by their otherworldly friend, Corporal Jared Scott. They'd grown used to his sudden appearances since they had first discovered him in their garden.

"Hello," he greeted them. "Another jamboree?" The ghost dog, Boo, sat at his feet.

Chucky laughed out loud and reached over to pat Boo's head. "You've seen enough of them to know," he said to the corporal, and the others nodded in agreement.

"Yes," Philip answered. The serious one, he felt an obligation to properly answer the corporal. "Dad's making mountain pies further down the hill." He pointed toward several fires down the slope. The sound of a band tuning up drifted on the wind, and in the early dusk they could see lines of campers trudging up the hills, in pairs, small groups, and singles. The jamborees were their most popular events. With music, and old-fashioned foods, and stories around campfires, they always brought out the best in folks. Attending a jamboree was one of Philip's favorite things about living on a campground.

Chucky patted Boo on the head and let his hand slide down the length of the beagle's long silky ears. "Mr. Nesbitt is supposed to stop by later tonight to tell Gettysburg ghost stories," he said. "We don't want to miss that!"

Zach elbowed him. "Speak for yourself! I'm not sure I can handle another ghost." He grinned at the corporal, who shook his head with a smile.

"What would you do without me, Zach?" the corporal asked. "Without me there would be no adventure in your life."

Zach shrugged, the grin still plastered on his face.

"Speaking of Gettysburg stories," Philip said, "maybe we could have a few stories of our own." He slid over, clearing a spot for Corporal Jared Scott to sit down.

"Yeah," Chucky agreed. "Tell us about what it was like during the days of the Civil War."

Casey stared at the spot they had cleared. She knew something was going on, and she figured, by the talk, that Corporal Scott had arrived. Since she was the only one of them that couldn't see him or hear him, she could only stare. "Is the corporal sitting there?" she whispered.

"Geez, you are such a dingbat, Casey." Chucky was clearly embarrassed by his sister. "Why are you whispering? The corporal can hear everything you say."

Casey giggled. "Oh, yeah. I guess he can. So, is he sitting there?"

Jared grinned, amused.

"Yes," Zach said. "He is sitting there. He's about to tell us stories about the wartime."

Chucky rolled his eyes. Why Zach liked Casey was beyond him!

Casey stared at the space beside Philip, wishing she could see the corporal like the boys did. She could see the ghost dog, Boo, at his feet, but not Corporal Jared Scott, and that bothered her. She stepped around Philip's log and sat down next to Zach.

"Don't be so rude, Casey," Chucky said. "You haven't even said hello to the corporal."

Casey giggled again. "Hi, Corp," she said. "We all want to hear your stories."

Jared Scott smiled, then stretched his long legs out in front of him, kicked a little dirt into the edge of the fire with a rough, worn boot, and put an arm behind him, palm down on the log. "Well, it was a tumultuous time," he said. "Most of the families were split, with the men off to war and the women at home doing the work of two."

"What did he say?" Casey interrupted. "I can't hear the corporal. I wish I could hear him."

"Sssh!" Chucky shushed his sister. "Zach, will you quietly repeat what the corporal says so we don't have to be interrupted by Casey all the time?"

"Sure." Zach smiled at Casey and moved closer so she would hear everything he said.

"The men had it hard," Jared said. "Marching for miles in shoes that were worn out, many of them barefoot, or wearing shoes stuffed with paper to pad the holes in the bottom. They were tired and weak from lack of rations. The rations we had were nothing to brag about. Eating hardtack was as close to eating a rock as I want to get. And every day seemed worse than the one before it."

Casey leaned close to Zach so she could hear the words he softly repeated.

"Some of us were luckier than others," Jared continued. "The cavalrymen had horses, and riding was easier. But we had to feed the brutes, and finding food for one was hard enough, let alone feeding two or more."

Jared swept an arm across the hill and beyond. "Gettysburg was bountiful though," he said. "In the orchards we found apples to pluck. It's true that many were green, but anything eatable was suitable fodder back then."

Casey snorted. "They should have let the women fight. Women would have known how to cut up a green apple and cook it into a fine green apple pie. They would have known how to mend the shoes and..." She stopped. "Why didn't they let women fight?" she asked.

For a moment, Jared looked stunned. "Women's work is in the kitchen," he said. "It's just the way of the world. Men hunt, and feed, and protect. Women nurture. Women have babies and care for families and...well...and cook."

After Zach repeated the corporal's words, Casey's mouth dropped open. "That's not the way it is anymore," she said indignantly. "Women make fine soldiers."

It seemed Jared was going to say something, but he stopped and instead looked thoughtful. "I do know this one woman," he said, "who fought in the war."

Now it was Chucky's turn to look surprised. "The Civil War? A woman? In the Civil War?"

"Yes, Chucky." Jared nodded. "I've seen her from time to time in the circle of friends that meet on the hill. I've heard murmurs about her past. They say she disguised herself as a man and enlisted. It wasn't until she was killed that anyone realized she was a woman." He shook his head. "Why in the world would a woman do something like that?"

For once, there was silence around the campfire. Even Casey was lost in thought. The fire crackled and spit as the flames grew smaller and the shadows grew longer.

Chucky was the most surprised. A woman who fought with the other soldiers in the Civil War! He'd never heard of that!

Then Casey sat up straight. "I wish I could talk to her." She turned to the space where Jared sat. "I'd like to meet her," she said.

Chucky stared at Casey, stunned. Her hair stuck up on the sides, she had a pair of pink plastic sunglasses hanging on a string around her neck, and her shorts didn't match her shirt. She would have looked comical if she didn't look so darned serious. "You can't meet her!" he said.

Casey put her hands on her hips and stared at her brother. "Why not? You have a ghost friend. Why can't I meet Jared's woman friend?"

Jared squirmed. "She's not my woman friend," he said. "She's just a woman I see with the guys on the hill from time to time. We've not even been properly introduced."

"I would love to meet her," Casey rushed on. "I would love to hear about the Civil War from a woman's viewpoint. I mean," she paused, "no offense, guys, but every story I've ever heard came from a guy. Women look at things differently." She turned toward Jared Scott. "I really want to meet her. Is there any way you could arrange it?"

The corporal was uncomfortable. He thought about the tortured look he'd seen in the woman soldier's eyes. But he could also hear how earnest Casey was. He had to agree that most of the information about the Civil War did come from men, passed down from the soldiers who had fought in it. "The next time we meet, I will talk to her," he said. "I will ask her if she will talk to a girl in the land of the living. I will tell her that you want to hear about the war from her. But..." He stared at Casey, who couldn't see the sad look in his eyes. Then he continued, "Just don't be surprised if she says no."

Chapter Two

Mr. Nesbitt's Ghosts

Casey didn't hear much more. As the conversation turned to Boo and the rabbits he'd been chasing, she stopped hearing the words and started thinking about Jared's friend. *What was I thinking, to ask the corporal if I could meet his ghost friend?* If she were honest with herself, she'd admit that sometimes she even wondered if the corporal really existed. She knew he was there of course, but she never actually saw him, so it was easy to imagine he was a product of the boys' imaginations. None of it seemed real to her. But she was certain that it would feel all too real if she went to Ghost Ring Hill to meet Jared's friend.

Chucky's hearty laugh made her jump. "Boo did what? Ran through a camper's tent trying to cut a rabbit off?"

"Yes," Philip said. "Isn't that what you said, Corporal? I wish I could have seen that man's face. Did he look scared?" He paused as he waited for the corporal to answer, then continued. "I knew he would! Ha, ha, ha!"

Chucky slapped his ball cap on his thigh and laughed again. Boo looked up at him, wiggling all over, wagging his tail and smiling that sloppy, tongue-hanging-out dog grin of his.

Casey shook her head. She could see Boo. She'd always been able to see the dog. So she knew Jared must be real too. And that meant his woman friend was real, too. *Oh, what have I gotten myself into?* she wondered.

"I just had a thought," Zach said suddenly. "I've seen Boo chasing after the real thing, but does he ever chase ghost rabbits?" He stopped, then went on. "He does? I knew it. I bet there are a lot of ghost rabbits up on Ghost Ring Hill."

Casey shivered. She'd heard the boys talk about the hill they'd dubbed Ghost Ring Hill after Jared had introduced them to a ring of ghostly friends in the dead of night. It had scared a camping ghost hunter named Skelly so much he'd checked out and left the campground in a huff. The way the boys talked, even they never wanted to go back again. And here she'd gone and asked to go up there with Jared! She shivered again.

Boo barked and Casey jumped at the hollow echoing sound of his voice. The dog raced off into the woods after something none of the friends at the campfire could see.

Philip stood up, looking at his watch. "We'd better hurry if we want to catch Mark Nesbitt's campfire stories." Philip kicked dirt into the dying embers, putting the campfire out. Zach and Chucky stood up, and Casey followed suit.

Corporal Jared Scott stretched his legs out a bit further. "I believe I'll sit here awhile and wait for that crazy cur to come back," he said. "You boys go on your way. Enjoy your stories." The boys watched the corporal as he smiled at Casey. "You too, young lady," he added.

Casey didn't move. She was still thinking about Ghost Ring Hill.

"The corporal said to tell you to enjoy the stories," Zach said.

"Bye, Corporal!" Casey waved and followed her brother and his two friends down the hill. She wasn't sure she was ready for any more ghost stories on this night.

* * * * *

"Hey Mr. Nesbitt," Zach called as they neared the bottom of the hill and the blazing fire they'd seen from above. He waved wildly, until Mark Nesbitt looked up from the marshmallow he was roasting, and saw Zach. He raised his hand in welcome, then fanned the hot, black marshmallow he had skewered on a sapling branch.

"Boys, come on over and make a toasted marshmallow. I like them black. How about you?"

Zach laughed. "That's too black for me," he said, reaching for a stick and the bag.

Casey watched. She didn't want a marshmallow. She wasn't sure she even wanted to be with the boys tonight. Home in her bed was starting to sound like a good idea, but it was too far to walk alone in the gathering dusk. So she sat down next to Zach on a log, just across from a heavyset man with four marshmallows threaded on his stick. Casey guessed he had come to hear Mr. Nesbitt's ghost stories, too.

Mr. Baxter introduced Mark Nesbitt to the campers. "Here's what you've all gathered for, to meet our famous local author. " He was animated, waving his arms toward Mr. Nesbitt with a flourish. "Mark Nesbitt has written five volumes of ghost stories, all gathered from eyewitness accounts. I am excited and proud to introduce to you, and to turn over the program to Mr. Nesbitt."

There was scattered applause from the large group of campers that sat on logs and in lawn chairs near the fire.

Mark licked a bit of marshmallow from his pinky finger and grinned at the audience boyishly. "Thank you," he said, his blue eyes dancing in the campfire light. "It is good to be here."

Casey took a deep breath. She always had bad dreams after seeing scary movies, and this time she was already scared, so she wasn't sure she should stay.

"Some say that Gettysburg is a hotbed of ghosts. Some say quite the opposite. They say there is no such thing as a ghost. I am here to tell you that they exist, that too many people have seen, and heard, and yes," he paused dramatically, "*felt* the presence of a ghost! How do we tell these people that they are all crazy? How do we discount their stories? I do not choose to discount them. I choose to tell them, and tonight I will share my favorite tales with you."

Casey slid down on the log, wrapping her arms around her knees.

Zach looked at Casey curiously, but only for a moment. His attention was on Mr. Nesbitt, whose arms were waving, casting shadows across the wavering firelight.

Casey blocked them out. She'd long ago learned how to block out Chucky's taunts and teases, and she used the method now to block out Mr. Nesbitt's stories. She focused on her toenails, bright pink and glowing from the light, and she imagined herself in her bedroom, painting the toes on each of her Barbie dolls, hot pink like her own. She heard the voice in the background, but every time a word came through she worked harder at blocking it out, until at last, all she heard was silence. Then she realized something. It really was silent.

The campers were all looking at Mark Nesbitt expectantly. He'd finished his storytelling.

"Now, do I have any questions?"

Casey listened as a few questions were asked. Then, timidly, she raised her hand.

"Yes." Mr. Nesbitt smiled at her brightly. "Casey, do you have a question?"

Casey stood up. "Did you ever hear about women soldiers serving in the war? Did you ever hear stories about the ghosts of women soldiers?"

There were some titters. Casey ignored them. Mr. Nesbitt would know. *Let them think I'm a silly girl,* she thought. *In a minute they'll find out that women did serve in the Civil War.*

Mr. Nesbitt didn't let her down. "Excellent question!" he answered, excitedly. "So few people know about the women who fought in the Civil War."

Now the people were quiet, leaning forward in their lawn chairs, listening.

"Some women disguised themselves as men and enlisted in the army." He hesitated. "I'm not sure why they did it, but they did. One woman, Sarah Edmonds Seelye of Flint Michigan, even worked as a spy for the Union!"

Everyone was quiet. Casey sat down, and leaned forward to hear better.

"She enlisted in the Michigan infantry, and called herself Frank Thompson. When the Union needed someone to disguise himself as a woman and infiltrate the Confederate troops, they chose good ol' Frank!" Mr. Nesbitt laughed. "Imagine how Sarah Seelye must have felt. Here she was, a woman who had fooled all those men, and now they wanted her to *dress up as a woman* and spy for them! And she did!"

Several listeners laughed.

Casey stood up again. "Were there others? Did any fight in Gettysburg?"

Mr. Nesbitt looked surprised. "Well, yes. There were many others, and yes, at least one fought at Gettysburg. But, to this day, we don't know who she was. Her body was found among the dead at Pickett's Charge. Her gender might never have been discovered if someone hadn't noticed she was a woman when they were preparing the graves."

Casey let out her breath in a whoosh. She was excited now. Women soldiers! It was a whole new thing to think about. Maybe she should work on getting rid of her fear. Maybe she should go meet Jared's friend and find out more.

Chapter Three

A Lesson in History

"Casey, come sit beside me."

The woman was tiny, with lines and wrinkles on her face. Her dress was long. It flowed over her knees and down to the top of her black, high-top shoes. Her dark brown hair was rolled in a bun, making her high cheekbones look sharp. She had kind eyes, and spoke so softly it was barely more than a whisper.

Casey heard the creaking of the rocking chair, and felt the breeze from it cross her bare legs. She shuddered and took a step backwards. Brown leaves crunched underfoot. "I don't know you," she said.

The woman smiled. "And I don't know you, my child, but I know that you want to hear my story. You've come to hear my story. Isn't that right?"

Casey looked around wildly, not understanding why she had come. Then she realized they were in the middle of a forest.

The woman looked sad. Her hands were folded quietly in her lap, but that rocking chair kept creaking back and forth, back and forth. Casey searched her mind. Where was she, and why had she come? She didn't know the answer.

Snap!

"Get up, Casey! Look how late you've slept!" Mom pulled the cord on Casey's second window shade, and it rose with another snap, letting even more sunlight pour into the room.

Casey opened her eyes and was assaulted by the light. The face on the alarm clock showed 9:00 a.m. She groaned and rolled over. A dream. It had all been a dream. But it had seemed so real.

"It's your morning to clean stalls at the stable. I've kept your breakfast warm. Come on now. You can do whatever you want this afternoon, but right now you need to get moving."

Casey threw the blanket over her face. "I'm up," she mumbled. "I promise, I'm up."

She heard Mom leave the room, and Casey slowly lowered the blanket. Where had that dream come from? she asked herself. But she knew it had come from Jared's stories about the woman. "My imagination is out of control," she said out loud, pushing the dream out of her head and forcing herself to put bare feet on the floor and stand. "Okay stable, here I come."

After the stables were cleaned, Casey went to look for the boys. She found them just behind the camp store, working in their garden.

Chucky huffed and pulled a large brown tomato plant out of the dirt. As the roots were released and it came out of the earth, dirt sprayed upward, hitting his bare legs. "Phew," Chucky said, as though pulling the plant had been major work. He pitched it into the basket beside him and looked up. "What do you want, Casey?"

Philip straightened from the beans he'd been pulling and piling, and Zach looked up, too.

"Hi, Casey," Zach grinned. "Where've you been?"

"I had to clean stalls today. I wondered where everyone was."

Zach pointed at his brother and rolled his eyes. "Our one day off from chores and Philip says we need to clean out the garden and get it ready for next spring. He practically insisted. He's such a slave driver!"

"I am not!" Philip's hands were on his waist. "We made a lot of money selling vegetables from this garden," he said. "You'd think you would want to take care of it for next year. It's just like you to be ungrateful!"

Chucky raised his hands, palms up. "Don't fight. We all knew when we planted it that we'd have to take care of our garden. Maybe we just need a break."

They sat with Casey on the edge of the garden.

"I had the strangest, most ghostly dream," Casey told them.

"Uh oh!" Zach threw his hands over his face. "Is this a family thing? The last time Chucky had a strange ghostly dream, it came true!"

Chucky's face turned red. "It doesn't run in this family," he said. "Casey always has wild dreams."

"I do not!"

Even though he wasn't past picking a fight with Philip, Zach didn't want Casey and Chucky to fight. "Whether you do or not doesn't matter," he said. "Just tell us, what did you dream?"

Casey turned to Zach. "I dreamed about a woman," she said, and then she told him the whole dream. "Why do you think I dreamed that?" she asked. "It was so real!"

Philip looked jittery. He pushed his glasses up on his nose. "You dreamed it because Jared's woman friend was on your mind. That's all there is to it. Not all dreams have to be prophetic, Zach."

Zach rolled his eyes. Philip and his big words! But he knew what Philip meant. "Not all dreams predict the future," he agreed, "but you never know."

"Let's get some lunch, then see if we can do some research," Philip said. "If Dad will take us to the library, maybe we can research women soldiers in the Civil War, and especially ones from this area. Maybe we'll find out something about Jared's friend."

"And if Dad can't take us to the library, maybe he will let us use the computer to do some Internet research."

Chucky stood up and brushed off the back of his pants. The junk in his pockets jingled. "That's a good idea," he said.

* * * * *

"Hey, here's that woman Mr. Nesbitt told us about!" Zach pointed at the computer screen. "It's an article in the *Winfield Courier, January 24, 1884* about Sarah Edmonds Seelye!" Zach's eyes moved rapidly, scanning the article.

"Read it out loud," Casey said. Even though it was only the four of them it felt like too many people were crowded around the computer.

"I'll read it," Philip said, sliding his chair over.

"This is Sarah's own words," Philip said. Now he sounded excited. "'A few weeks before I left home, my father took it into his head to marry me off, and get rid of me. In obedience to his orders, I became engaged, but while the preparations were going on for the wedding, one starless night, I unceremoniously left for parts unknown.'"

"I wonder how old she was?" Chucky said.

"I don't know," Zach answered, "but it says she dressed as a man to get a job and went door to door selling Bibles."

Philip stared at Zach, whose eyes were back on the screen, reading ahead again.

"Hmmm, so she dressed as a man even before becoming a soldier," Chucky said.

"It says she got married after she served in the army," Zach added.

"Did she ever serve in the army around here?" Casey asked. She was still thinking about her ghost, the one she planned to meet.

"Not that I see," Zach said.

"Then let's look somewhere else," Philip said. "Sarah is not our ghost."

"I wish Dad could have taken us to the library," Zach said.

"Me too," Philip agreed. "He said maybe he would on Saturday."

Zach was back to the search screen.

"Put in *Female soldiers, Gettysburg*," Chucky said, and Zach did.

He clicked on a link, then read. "'Despite the fact that the U.S. Army did not acknowledge or advertise their existence, it is surprising that the women soldiers of the Civil War are not better known today. After all, their existence was known at the time and through the rest of the nineteenth century.'"

"Wow!" Philip pushed his glasses up on his nose. "Wonder why we don't all know about it?"

"Once again, the woman is the unsung hero!" Casey said dramatically.

Zach continued scanning the article. "Hey! Listen to this! 'One anonymous woman wearing the uniform of a Confederate private was found dead on the Gettysburg battlefield on July 17, 1863, by a burial detail from the Union II Corps. Based on the location of the body, it is likely the Southern woman died participating in Pickett's charge.'"

Suddenly, Casey felt numb. "That's the woman Mark Nesbitt mentioned. The one found at Pickett's charge. She wasn't a Union soldier. She was a Southern woman, far from home, her body never identified. Her family must have worried about her for the rest of their lives, not knowing where she was, or if she was safe, or dead, or alive."

Hearing it made it seem so real. It made Casey wonder again...was this the woman Jared knew?

Chapter Four

Casey Chickens Out

The evening breeze was cooler than it had been in awhile. The leaves were bright with color, reminding the boys that school was just around the corner. They walked along the campground trail, stopping at each soda machine so Philip could empty the change and see which sodas needed to be filled, writing notations in his pocket-size notebook.

"Man, I can't believe summer is almost over," Zach said.

"It seems like school just ended," Chucky agreed.

"That's true," Philip said, "but think about everything that has happened this summer! We dug up an I.D. tag and met a ghost friend, we helped reunite a ghost boy with his family, we found a ghost horse, and stopped a ghost hunter from scaring away all the ghosts in Gettysburg. It's as if we opened the doors to another world!"

"It does seem like it," Zach said. "And don't forget the ghost at Aunt Penny's house!"

"On the normal side of things, we grew a garden and sold the produce," Chucky added. "You know, I bet we've earned enough to buy that Swiss camping knife we wanted." He hesitated. "Are we ever going to buy that knife?"

Philip stopped walking. "We have all that money in the cigar box. What are we going to do with it? Do you guys still want to buy it? We definitely have enough money now."

"It *is* a cool knife," Zach said.

"It's triple-cool," Chucky said softly. "But do you still want the knife? I mean, who would keep it anyway? We'd have to pass it around." He stuck his hands in his pockets, and leaned against a picnic bench, jiggling the junk in his pockets.

"I never was interested in the knife," Philip said.

"I wanted it then, but now it doesn't seem so important," Zach said.

Both boys looked at Chucky.

"You still want the knife, don't you, Chucky?"

"It's an awful cool knife. It has a knife, and a fork, and a corkscrew, a screwdriver, all kinds of gadgets," he reminded them.

Philip and Zach grinned.

"Let's count the money up and see how much we have," Philip said. "We had almost forty dollars the last time I counted it, and I know there's more than that now. We could get one big thing to share, or split it up."

"If we split it, you can get your knife, Chucky!" Zach said.

"Remember, we have to put aside enough to buy seeds and plants to start next year's garden," Philip said. "We have to show Dad we are good businessmen."

Zach laughed, and they walked on. "Hey Chucky, where's Casey today?" he asked.

"Heck, I don't know. I try to stay away from her as much as I can."

"I like Casey," Zach said.

Chucky rolled his eyes. "Geez, Zach, you gotta learn to be more particular about the women you like."

Zach blushed. "It's not like that!"

"She is different now," Philip said. "Casey's growing up or something. She's not a bratty little kid anymore."

"Hmmph. That's what you think. You don't have to live with her."

"Well, she sure is serious about this ghost woman," Philip said.

"Yes, and it is awful brave of Casey to ask to meet her. I mean..." Zach stopped. "I'd never volunteer to meet a ghost I didn't know."

The boys stopped talking as they rounded the bend in the road. Each was thinking about the ghost soldier, wondering why Casey wanted to meet with her. Then, there was Casey, right in the middle of the road, on one knee with her arms around Boo.

"Speak of the devil," Chucky said.

Casey jumped up. "Hey guys. I wondered where you were. Did you see Boo is here? Is Jared here too?" She peered into the bushes along the trail.

Philip looked, too. "Nope, just Boo."

"I think he's been hunting rabbits." Casey let go of Boo and stood up.

"Real ones, or ghost ones?" Chucky's eyes danced.

Casey faked a shiver. "Real, I hope!"

"You can't be afraid of a ghost rabbit," Zach said. "After all you are going to meet that woman soldier and she's a lot bigger than a little ol' rabbit."

Casey's expression changed rapidly. Her eyes were wide. "Maybe I shouldn't have told Jared that," she said. "I've been thinking. Maybe I should just forget the whole idea. At first, I wanted to meet her. She could help us see the Civil War through a woman's eyes. But now, I just don't know..." Her voice trailed off.

Philip patted her shoulder. "Don't worry. Maybe Jared hasn't spoken to her yet. Or maybe she won't want to meet with you anyway. Then, you can chicken out gracefully."

Casey stuck her chin up and walked beside Philip, hoping he was right.

"Don't you have something to do, Casey?"

Chucky's words stopped Casey in mid-step. "Yeah, but I wanted to be with you guys too." Her cracking voice and the way she lowered her eyes reflected the hurt she felt. "But, if you want to be alone..."

"Chucky!" Zach elbowed Chucky. "Don't be so mean. Casey's not bothering us."

Chucky glanced at Philip, then rolled his eyes. "She's bothering me."

"It's okay," Casey said. "I have to take Prissy for a walk anyway." Her shoulders drooped as she turned around and headed toward the house.

Zach's face was hot. "That was really mean, Chucky!" he blurted. "And don't even start rolling your eyes and acting like she's my girlfriend or something. She's not! But she is my friend, and anyone would tell you that that was just plain mean!"

The grin melted from Chucky's face and a stunned look moved into place. "I didn't mean to make you mad, Zach. But I get tired of her hanging around."

"Maybe she's lonely. Maybe you should think about that."

Philip cleared his throat. "Come on guys, don't fight." He looked uncomfortable. "Let's go back to the store and count the money we have in the cigar box."

"Sure, Philip. That's a good idea," Chucky said.

Zach just grunted, but he followed them down the trail.

* * * * *

That evening, they sprawled on the grassy bank on one side of the garden, looking at the rows of brown dirt, eyeing the few weeds poking up. "That garden sure was good to us," Philip said. "One hundred forty-seven dollars! We never thought we'd make that much, did we?"

Zach hooted. "It's more money than we ever made before!"

Chucky punched Zach in the arm and grinned. He was agreeing with Zach about everything, trying to make up for making his friend so upset. "And it harvested us a ghost!" he added.

Just as he said the word *ghost,* he felt a chill.

"I was not harvested from your garden." Jared smiled.

All three boys scrambled to their feet.

"Hi, Jared." Chucky looked like he wanted to salute.

"Hello, boys. Where is Casey?"

Chucky shrugged and looked down at his sneakers.

"Probably inside with her dog, Prissy," Zach said.

"I was hoping to talk to her tonight. Since she is not here, will you give her a message from me?"

"Sure, Corporal." Philip was the first to speak, but Chucky and Zach were nodding, too.

"Tell her that my friend said she would meet with her. She is hoping Casey will help her find some information." Jared looked sad. "Maybe Casey can finally put Mrs. Daniel's mind at ease."

Chapter Five

Meeting Althea

"Gee, I don't want to be the one to tell Casey." Zach shook his head sadly. "Now it will really be hard for her to chicken out."

"Girls! They're a bunch of bawl-babies." Chucky pulled a tiny compass out of his pocket and fiddled with it. "Why are they so afraid of everything?"

"Yeah, Chucky. You were never afraid, right?" Zach grinned at Philip. "You were so brave every time we saw a ghost. Such a hero, you were!"

Philip didn't want to smile, but he felt it spreading across his face just the same. In his mind, he could see the look on Chucky's face the first time the corporal had appeared, and again, the day they met the ghost horse on the trail. Remembering it fueled his smile, and even after he saw the red spread across Chucky's face he couldn't stop.

Chucky stood up. "We might as well go find Casey," he said abruptly. "The sooner we tell her, the better."

* * * * *

Casey was in the stable, leading the mare Sugar out of her stall. Zach waved and smiled and Casey paused a moment, stroking Sugar's spotted neck.

"What are you guys doing here?" She seldom saw the boys hanging around the stable.

Chucky patted the pony's nose and she lowered her head to him. Sugar was his favorite pony. "We came to talk to you," he said.

"Oh, well, just give me a moment to let her go," Casey said. The boys watched as she walked to the lower lot and turned the little Appaloosa out.

"You tell her, Philip," Zach said. "I just can't bring myself to do it."

Philip ran a hand through his hair, then pushed his glasses back up on his nose. "It's always me."

Behind Casey, Sugar whinnied. Casey smiled. "See ya, Sugar," she said, then looked expectantly at the boys. "What's up?"

Chucky smiled. Zach looked nervous.

Philip jumped right in. "Jared came to the garden looking for you," he said.

Casey's smile faded and concern filled her eyes. "Did you tell him not to ask..."

"No," Philip jumped right in. He knew what she was going to say. "Jared had already talked to his friend, and she wants to meet you. He said maybe you can put her mind at ease, whatever that means."

Casey's expression crumbled. She looked down at her black barn boots and sighed. "I should have found the corporal earlier."

"What will you do?" Zach looked worried.

"I'll go meet her," Casey said. "I have to. I said I would."

* * * * *

They gathered at the garden the very next night. It was one of those nights when the sky looked as big as Texas, and full of brightly twinkling stars. It was perfect, since Philip had told Mr. Baxter that they were going out to watch for satellites. The air was crisp, with a hint of early autumn on the breeze that ruffled Casey's ponytail. The corporal was to meet them there at 9:00 p.m.

Casey shivered and rubbed her bare arms. "I didn't bring a sweater," she said.

Zach touched her arm. "You are cold," he said. He thought it was not the air that made her feel cold, but the fear she must be feeling.

They heard the corporal whistling before they saw him come down the camp lane. "Lovely night, my friends, isn't it?"

"Yes it is," Chucky answered quickly, and the others nodded.

"Althea will expect us shortly, so let's be off," the corporal said.

Casey fell into line with the boys to follow Jared toward the field, and up the incline to Ghost Ring Hill. *Althea.* It was the first time she'd heard him say her name. She shivered again, remembering the lady in her dream. She half-expected to see a rocking chair sitting in the middle of the woods when they got there, just like in the dream.

As they entered the cool, dark wooded section with the path cutting up the hill, Chucky started jiggling the junk in his pockets again. It was a habit Casey wished he would break, especially now, with the jiggling objects rattling in his pockets and cutting through the quiet night air, sounding louder than ever.

"Chucky, ssshh!" Zach finally said what Casey had been thinking.

"I'm a little nervous," Chucky confessed. "Do we have to be there when Casey meets her, or can we stay back, away from the clearing?"

Jared smiled. "You can stay back. In fact, I'd prefer that you let Casey talk to Althea alone. She has some things she needs to get off her chest."

Chucky sighed a sigh of relief, but Casey's heartbeat stepped up. Before she could say anything, they'd reached the top of the hill and the path widened, coming out into the clearing at the top.

Jared stood still, as though listening, then he spoke. "Althea is to meet us here. You boys can wait under the trees, like you did the time we had the meeting with Skelly." A smile crossed his lips as he spoke of the time they'd brought the ghost hunter, Skelly, to Ghost Ring Hill.

"Sure thing, Corporal," Chucky said, as he chose a tree to lean against.

"You can come with me," Jared told Casey.

"Jared says you can follow him to the clearing," Philip said.

Casey nodded nervously and walked out into the opening, hoping she was going in the right direction. She glanced back at the boys and saw Zach giving her two thumbs up. She listened hard, then followed the crunching sound of Corporal Jared Scott's footsteps, wishing one more time that she could at least see the ghost soldier she had grown to trust.

The corporal stopped in the center of the clearing. Casey took a few more steps, then felt Jared tug at her collar, signaling for her to stop. She stood in the center of the meadow, at the highest part of the campground, feeling very alone, and waited. "Jared?" Her voice was timid.

Casey listened, then she heard a voice, but it wasn't Jared.

"Casey? Is that your name, child? Are you Casey?"

Casey spun around, half expecting to see a woman in a rocking chair. She was startled to see a fuzzy outline standing to her left. She was short, only a little taller than Casey herself. Her dress was long, touching the leaves and vines that stretched upward in the dusty moonlight. The front of her dress looked like a tuxedo, with white frills, and a bowtie at her neck, and her middle was cinched in as though a belt were at her waist.

Casey tried to bring the woman into focus, but her shape shifted and wobbled like a scrambled picture on a television set.

"Yes," Casey's voice quivered. "I am Casey."

"You wanted to meet me?"

Casey was taken by the hollow sound of her voice, but she nodded just the same.

"What is it that made you want to talk with me?" The voice seemed stronger, and the image less fuzzy. Now Casey could see the steel gray eyes, and the way they looked right at her.

"I...everyone...well..." Casey had trouble finding her voice. "Everyone tells stories about the Civil War, but no one ever talks about the women that fought." Her words came out in a rush. "I wanted to know more about *why* women went to war, and what they did for their country."

The ghost woman looked deep into Casey's eyes, and Casey could not look away. Suddenly Casey's chest felt like a weight was on it, and an overwhelming sadness filled her.

"There were many reasons women fought," Althea said slowly. Her voice was heavy with pain. "But my reason for running off to war was wrong. I lost so much because of my own pain and anger. I gave up so much."

Casey couldn't take her eyes off the ghost, who was starting to fade, the sound of her voice getting thinner with every word.

"We must talk, Casey. You can help me find peace."

She was fading fast. Casey watched her go from a figure she could see, into a shifting form, colored mist, and then a fog that disappeared. She stood still, staring at the spot where the woman had been until Jared took her arm. She was surprised that she could feel the brush of wind on her arm and know that it was Jared.

"Tell her that Althea is gone," he said softly, and Philip stepped forward to repeat Jared's words to Casey.

Still Casey stared at the spot where Althea had stood. *So much sadness. So much pain.* Casey felt as though it were her own. *But why? What had caused Althea so much hurt?*

"Casey." Zach was beside her. "Are you okay?"

Casey shook away the heaviness that sat on her heart, and looked at Zach. "I'm okay, Zach. Really, I am. But Althea is not. I have to find out what is causing her so much pain. We have to help her." Casey's voice sounded desperate.

She followed the boys from the clearing. The words Althea had said were like pieces to a puzzle, disjointed and hard to fit together. Casey shook her head sadly. In her heart, she knew she had to see Althea again, had to find out what had happened and what she could do to help. She needed the missing pieces to put the puzzle together and try to bring peace to Althea.

Chapter Six

Althea's Story

The walk from Ghost Ring Hill back to the campground seemed much shorter than it had on the way up. Casey's mind raced ahead of her, wondering what she could do for Althea, and why the soft-spoken woman thought Casey could make a difference.

"Jared?" Casey said as they walked along the camp lane toward the garden. "Do you know what happened to Althea, and what she wants me to do?" She looked at Zach expectantly. She knew he would repeat the corporal's words to her.

"No. Althea has never shared her story with us. It seems it is too painful. I'm not sure why she believes you can help her. Perhaps it is because you are a woman too, a woman on the living side."

Casey's chest puffed up as Zach repeated the corporal's words. Not just because she was the first person Althea wanted to confide in, but also because

Jared had called her a woman. "What do I do next?" she asked.

Zach smiled at Casey as he listened to the corporal's reply. "Jared says she will meet with you again. It is hard for her to make herself solid enough to be seen. It's something that takes a lot of time to learn and Althea's had little practice. She was too tired to go on."

"Oh." Casey followed the boys up the gravel path, watching the moonlight spill across the road with patches of shade and light, and how the fluorescent pink shoelaces on her sneakers turned bright each time they hit the light. *So that was why Althea had turned to mist and drifted away.* It would be hard waiting and not doing anything until they met again. "When will we see her again?"

"Tomorrow night," Zach said, repeating the corporal's words. "Jared says Althea is anxious to talk to you again."

Chucky and Philip had been quiet on the walk down the road. Now Chucky said, "Should we come along, too?"

"It's up to you," Jared answered. "But I'm sure Casey would like your support."

"Why wouldn't you want to come?" Casey asked, surprised.

Philip pushed his glasses up on his nose. "We want to come," he said, jabbing Chucky with an elbow. "It's just that we can't see or hear anything."

Casey's mouth dropped open. "You couldn't see Althea, or hear when she talked to me?"

Chucky, Philip, and Zach all shook their heads. "Nope," Chucky said for all of them.

"Casey is the one that connects with her," Jared said. "That is why she is the only one who hears and sees her. As Althea learns more about how to project herself, her image will get stronger and you will be able to see and hear her, too."

They walked along in silence for awhile. When they reached the garden, the corporal bid them farewell, fading away into the night.

"What did she look like?" Zach asked.

"She wore a long dress with a frilly front," Casey answered. "Her hair was rolled into a tight bun on the top of her head, and her eyes..." Casey stopped, feeling that overwhelming sadness settle over her again as she thought of the steel gray eyes that had pierced her soul. "Her eyes were blue-gray," she forced herself to finish. She put her head on Zach's shoulder, fighting the urge to cry. "She is so sad," she told the boys. "You can't imagine how sad she is, and she made me feel it, too." She looked up at the boys, fighting the tears that wanted to erupt. "We have to help her," she said. "No matter what it takes."

* * * * *

At eight o'clock Sunday evening, they met Corporal Scott at the garden for the trek up the path to Ghost Ring Hill. Casey was tired. She'd slept fitfully the night before, dreaming of Althea, seeing her in Union colors in the dream.

"Dad wondered why we were going out to look for satellites two nights in a row," Philip said.

"What did you tell him?" Chucky asked.

"We just pointed at that sky full of stars and told him that two perfect nights in a row were awesome, too much to ask for!" Zach laughed. "We're lucky tonight is the same as last night!"

Chucky laughed. "That was triple-lucky!" he said.

Casey walked behind them at a slower pace. She couldn't shake the sad feeling, or the notion that a kid like her would not be able to make things better. Just what could she, a nine-year-old girl, do for Althea?

"Come on, Casey," Chucky said. "You're holding us up."

Casey picked up her step. "I'm just tired," she said. "I didn't sleep very well last night."

"Did you dream again?" Zach dropped back to walk beside her.

"Yes. All night." She perked up. "Ask Jared if Althea fought for the Union, or the Confederates."

"Union," Jared said, and Zach repeated it.

Casey gasped, and the boys stopped walking.

"What?" Philip asked.

"I dreamed of her in uniform, her bun tucked up tightly under a Union cap." Casey shivered. "I can't believe I dreamed that and it was true."

Chucky whistled. "Cool," he said. "Triple-cool."

"You have made a connection with Althea," Jared said. "That is why you are having premonitions, and dreams that are telling."

Zach repeated the corporal's words, stopping on the word *premonition.* "What does that mean?" he asked.

"It means that Casey is getting feelings about things that are true, or will come true," Philip said.

"Oh."

"We're almost there," the corporal said, as they came out of the copse of trees at the top. "You boys want to wait back here again?"

"Will you wait with us?" Chucky asked.

"If Casey feels brave enough to go out into the opening alone," the corporal answered.

"Casey, can Jared stay back with us?" Chucky asked.

Casey barely heard Chucky's words. She was staring at the clearing, and at Althea, who waited, sitting on a log on the other side. Her dark navy dress flowed over her knees and down to the ground, her head was buried in her arms, resting on her knees. She looked so sad.

"I'm fine," she said, and walked across the clearing to Althea, to hear the story she needed to hear.

Althea raised her head as Casey approached. She smiled, and even her smile seemed forced, small and sad.

Casey settled on the log beside her. The ghost woman had worked hard at coming out, Casey could tell. She was much more solid than she had been the night before. Her face was creamy white and clear, and those eyes...those eyes looked right into Casey.

Casey lost all of her fear. She reached across and took Althea's hand. At first, she felt nothing, but then the wispy mist became solid and Casey gripped the hand tighter. "Tell me your story," she said.

Althea smiled again, and looked down at her lap. Then she began.

"John and I were so happy," she said. "We had just built our first home. The whole community helped us raise it up. We had a son, William, and he was the apple of John's eye. Things were perfect. Then the war broke out. William was only a year and a half old when John marched out with the 5th Pennsylvania Infantry. He promised me he would come back and everything would be okay."

Althea stopped, pushing away a tear.

Casey watched the tear roll down Althea's face, crystal clear and as sparkling as a liquid diamond.

"But he didn't come back. He was killed on William's second birthday."

The words hung on the air like dead weight. Casey felt tears forming behind her own eyes as she waited for Althea to continue.

"I was grief-stricken. I couldn't think of anything but how those rebels had killed my Johnny. I lost sight of everything that was important to me. Grief consumed me until I couldn't think straight. I ran off, leaving William behind with my mother, in Westminster." Althea buried her head in her arms and sobbed. "I didn't realize that William was all I had left of my Johnny."

"I cut my hair short, disguised myself as a man, changed my name to Al Daniels, and enlisted in the very same unit my Johnny had died for. I wanted to kill those rebels. I wanted to give them what they deserved for killing my husband, for ruining my life."

Casey squeezed Althea's hand, but could not feel it.

"I left behind the only thing I had left in life, William." She was speaking between sobs now, and her figure was getting thinner, turning to mist.

"Did you stay in the army?" Casey rubbed Althea's shoulder, but it slid into pieces of mist beneath her hands. Casey watched in horror.

"I was killed, just like my Johnny. The rebels took me down."

Casey swallowed hard. She put her hands in her lap, watching her new friend fall apart, and wishing she could help Althea feel good again.

"Please find out what happened to my William," Althea said. "I will never be able to rest unless I know."

Casey nodded. "I'll help," she said. "I'll try to find out what happened to your son." Casey was confused and promising things she did not know she could do. How would she find information about William?

"His name was William John Daniels, III," Althea said. "Find him. Please."

She faded even more, becoming a blotchy mist, and then drifted away. Casey watched her go, like clouds drifting in an open sky, and wondered how she would ever be able to keep her promise.

Chapter Seven

Searching for William

Casey sat on the log and stared at the space where Althea had been.

"Wow! That was wild, how she just faded away like that. Not like you, Corp. She kind of broke into pieces and drifted off! Wowie zowie." Zach was racing toward Casey. He couldn't contain his excitement.

"You could see her?" Casey's voice was small.

"Heck, yeah," Zach said. "We could see her alright. Jared said she's been working on projecting herself." He grinned. "I've never seen a woman ghost before."

Casey couldn't bring herself to smile back at him. "She is so sad. She lost everything, and then lost her life. She wants me to find out about her son, William, but I don't know where to start. Now what do I do?"

"We'll start at the library," Philip said. "That's where we found out about Jared's cavalry friend."

"It will be fun," Zach added. "Aunt Penny said to call her and we would go out somewhere this week. Maybe she can take us tomorrow."

"Come on," Chucky said. A breeze was starting to pick up and he was impatient. "Let's get home."

Casey stood up, looking for Althea. The clouds had faded and the night air was shifting as though a storm was coming on. She saw no sign of her ghost friend. "Is Jared here?" she asked nervously.

"I am," he said, and Zach repeated it. Then, together they started down the hill, Casey's stomach rumbling and her mind racing.

* * * * *

Aunt Penny picked them up at 10:00 a.m. the next morning. She'd been excited when they called. She told Zach that she missed having them at the house. Only a few weeks before, they'd stayed with her at her Gettysburg home to help her move in. She was young, and fun, and the boys loved spending time with her.

"The library," she said, as the boys buckled their seat belts. Casey sat up front with Aunt Penny. "It's good to see you out with the boys," she told Casey. "What do you plan to find at the library?"

Casey looked back at the boys, not knowing how to answer.

"Well, we want to find out about someone who lived during the Civil War," Zach answered. Aunt Penny was cool. She'd known about the ghost in her own house, and although they'd never really talked about the boys seeing ghosts, he suspected she knew.

"Anyone in particular?"

Philip cleared his throat and pushed his glasses up on his nose. "His name is William John Daniels, III. His dad and mom were killed in battles around 1863. He was only two years old, then. We want to find out what happened to him."

Chucky looked nervous. Philip and Zach were talking too much.

"What makes you want to research this guy?" Aunt Penny looked over her shoulder as she drove onto the Baltimore Road. Her ponytail swung as she turned to look at them.

"We're helping a friend," Philip said.

Aunt Penny opened her mouth as though to ask another question, then closed it again. "Okay," she said. "Let's see what we can find."

Chucky let out the breath he was holding. He loved Aunt Penny. She knew just when to stop asking questions.

Casey squirmed in her seat. *They'd never be able to find out about William and what he did with his life. They didn't even know where to start!* But then, she looked back at Philip, who seemed so calm, doodling in the margin of his spiral notebook as they rode toward town. If anyone could find out, it was Philip.

In the library, Philip went right to the reference desk to ask for help.

"Where would I find information about someone who lived in Maryland, during the Civil War?" he asked.

"Civil War books are in the 900s," the librarian told him with a smile. She pointed to the nonfiction section.

"Yes, but..." Casey wanted to explain what they needed, but she stopped. *How do you explain that you are looking for someone you know nothing about?* Before Casey could form the words she needed, the reference librarian moved toward another patron and the opportunity was lost.

"Hey, I like your Chicago Bears cap," a young girl said to Chucky. "My uncle lives in Chicago and he wears the same hat."

Casey and the boys looked at the girl, who carried a dripping watering can.

"Oh." She held the can high. "I'm a library volunteer," she explained. "Today is my day to water the plants. What are you looking for?"

Casey smiled. She was drawn to the friendly girl with the frizzy blonde ponytail. She was tall and wore glasses, and shorts with a Girl Scout camp T-shirt with a name over the pocket. "Thanks, Livy," she said, trying out the name. "We want to find out what happened to a kid that lived during the time of the Civil War."

"A specific kid?"

"Yes." Casey smiled. Even if this girl was only a few years older than she was, at least someone was listening.

"Is it someone you knew?"

Philip looked impatient. "My grandparents knew the family," he lied. "I'm sure we can find something in the 900s section." He moved in that direction, but Casey stayed.

"All we really know is that the child's name was William John Daniels, III. He was a child during the Civil War and probably grew up in Carroll County, Maryland, with his grandparents, since both his parents were killed in the war." Casey paused. "See how hard this is going to be?"

Livy looked excited. She set down the watering can. "I really think I can help you!" she exclaimed so loudly that the librarian at the desk gave her a sharp look. "My Aunt Sue is a genealogist and she works for the Carroll County Historical Society. She loves this kind of a mystery!"

Zach hovered behind Casey. He had not followed Philip and Chucky when they'd wandered away to the nonfiction section. Now he grinned at Livy.

Casey's eyes lit up. "Do you really think she would help us?"

"Sure she will. Let me get some paper."

Livy hurried to get a short pencil and a scrap of paper by the computer terminals. Strands of frizzy blonde hair had escaped the rubber band in her hair, and they bobbed up and down as she moved, peering over her glasses to write something on the paper.

"She's really going to help us," Casey said to Zach.

"Wait till Philip finds out that he walked away from the best research, and no matter how smart he is, you got the best lead!" he laughed.

"Here you go!" Livy shoved a piece of paper in Casey's hand.

Casey looked down. The paper said, "Aunt Sue Bundy." Beside the name was a telephone number and an email address.

"You'll love my Aunt Sue, and she'll love you." Then she repeated what she'd said once before. "Aunt Sue loves a good mystery."

Chapter Eight

One Step Forward

Casey was so excited she almost hugged Livy before they left the library. Instead, she gripped the paper tight in her hand and thought about how it might help Althea.

In the car, they told Aunt Penny about meeting Livy. "They say there are no accidents," she said. "Who would have thought you'd meet just the person who could lead you in the right direction?"

Zach patted Chucky's head. "And all because she noticed Chucky's ball cap!"

Casey buckled her seat belt. "Whatever the reason, I'm just glad we were all there at the right time." She read the name on the paper again. *Sue Bundy. Will you really be able to help Althea, and me?* she wondered.

"Philip, can we email this lady from your house?"

"I guess so," Philip said. He was still thinking about how he and Chucky had come back from the

900s shelves to find the others grinning with that volunteer.

"You're not going home already," Aunt Penny said as she pulled away from the curb. "I wanted to spend some time with all of you. So how would you like to get lunch fixings and come to my house? Casey, you can use my computer to email that lady."

They all agreed, and Casey leaned forward to put the paper into the glove compartment. She wasn't going to take any chances on losing the paper in the grocery store.

They bought lunch meat, and cheese, fruit salad, and milk.

When they got to Aunt Penny's house, Casey spoke up. "It's my search, and I'll tell you if you really want to know, but I don't know if you'll believe me." Casey looked up at Aunt Penny and waited for her to answer.

Aunt Penny glanced at the boys, then back at Casey. "I have a feeling this has something to do with a ghost. Am I right?"

Philip's mouth dropped open.

Aunt Penny held a hand up in the air. "No need to say more. I do hope we can all talk about this at some point." She hesitated. "This, and what happened when I first moved in here."

Chucky looked at Philip and Zach. They weren't surprised that she knew they knew, just surprised she would say it out loud!

Aunt Penny smiled. "But right now I think I'll just get those extra cookies." With that, she walked past Chucky and into the kitchen. Chucky turned to follow her.

"I think we should tell her everything," Zach whispered. "She'd believe us, and she wouldn't tell Dad if we asked her not to."

"You're right," Philip agreed. He could hear Aunt Penny and Chucky digging cookies out of the package. "Casey, if you can do the email by yourself, we can go in there and tell her now."

Zach nodded. "Let's do it."

"Go ahead," Casey said. "I know just what I want to write."

The boys followed Chucky and Aunt Penny into the kitchen.

Casey clicked on *New Message*. She typed in Sue Bundy's email address. In the subject line she wrote, *Livy said to ask you.* Casey thought she'd be more likely to open the email and read it if she saw Livy's name.

Dear Sue Bundy,

My name is Casey Coppersmith. Today I met your niece, Livy, in the Gettysburg Public Library. She is very nice. I was looking to find out about someone who lived during the Civil War. When Livy heard me say Carroll County, Maryland, she gave me your email address and said that you love a mystery. Maybe you can help me with this one.

I need to find out what happened to William John Daniels III, who was born around 1861. His father, John (probably William John), and his mother, Althea, both died during the war. He went to live with his grandmother in Westminster, Maryland. I'm not sure which set of grandparents they were, but I think they were Althea's parents.

I know this isn't much to go on, but any help you can give us would be great. This address is to my friend's aunt's house. You can write me here. Thank you so much!

Your Friend,

Casey Coppersmith

"I hope this works out, Althea," Casey whispered as she typed the address at the bottom of the note. Then she clicked *SEND*.

Once the letter had disappeared and her message was out there in space somewhere on its way to a stranger, Casey's insides trembled a little. How often did the lady check her email? How long until she found the message and read it? Should she have told Aunt Sue that she could call Livy to find out that she was real, and they had really talked? So many thoughts swirled inside of her.

Casey got up and went into the kitchen where Aunt Penny and the boys were at the table, a plate of cookies and a jug of milk in the center.

Zach was talking and laughing at the same time. "We thought for sure that he'd come flying off when that deer jumped in front of you and you had to slam on the brakes!"

Aunt Penny put her hand up to her mouth, then she saw Casey. "Are you finished?"

"Yes, thanks. I hope she writes back," Casey said. "Who flew off what?"

"The boys are telling me about Jared and how he rode all the way here on the roof of my car!"

"I never heard that story!" Casey looked at the boys expectantly. When they didn't offer any information, she went on. "I can't see Jared," she said sadly. "Only the boys and Mr. Nesbitt can see him." Casey made her way to the table. She grabbed a chocolate chip cookie. "I wonder why Jared can't make me see him? Althea lets me see her, and even the boys saw her."

"Althea?" Aunt Penny's eyebrows rode high. "There's another ghost called Althea?"

"We hadn't gotten to that yet," Philip said.

Aunt Penny patted the chair beside her. "Well, do sit down, Casey. You must tell me more."

* * * * *

Later, Aunt Penny took them home. Chucky and Casey thanked her and waved, then headed to their little house behind the camp store.

Mr. Baxter had just started making supper when Zach, Philip, and Aunt Penny came in. "I was beginning to think I was going to have to eat all by myself," he said with a smile. "Penny, will you stay for spaghetti?"

"Sure thing. Do you need any help?"

"No. Just sit. You've had the kids all day. Was it fun?"

"We had a great time," she said.

"We went to the library, then got groceries and had lunch at Aunt Penny's house," Zach told his dad.

"I didn't get to eat lunch today," Mr. Baxter said. "So, I'm hungry. Boys, get the garlic bread out of the freezer and put it into the oven."

* * * * *

Chucky and Casey's mom was in the middle of cooking dinner when they walked in. She had meatloaf, mashed potatoes, and green beans for dinner. Chucky had never liked green beans, until he grew them in their own garden. Thinking of the garden made him think of his share of the money they'd made selling produce in the camp store, and the cool knife he was going to buy with it. Once he had that knife he'd eat dinner with it every night!

Casey watched her mom take the meatloaf out of the oven. She tried to picture her mother in a soldier's uniform. She couldn't do it, and when she stopped trying, Althea popped into her mind. Casey absentmindedly gave Prissy a chunk of meatloaf off her plate.

"Casey," her mom cried. "Please don't give the dog food from the table."

"I'm sorry. I wasn't thinking."

Just then, the poodle stood up on her hind legs, holding her front paws out in front of her. Even Mrs. Coppersmith smiled.

"She is cute," she said.

Chucky looked away. *Cute*? Prissy wasn't a *real* dog. She was so girly, it made him want to gag!

"Give her some dog food in her bowl," Mrs. Coppersmith said. "I keep forgetting to feed her before we eat."

Casey went to the sink and opened the cabinet beneath to get the bag of dog kibble. As she straightened, her gaze was drawn out the window toward the hills that rose up from the campground. *Was Althea out there? Was she waiting for word?*

Prissy jumped up against Casey's leg. "Okay, girl," Casey baby-talked to her fluffy, little dog. "Here you go." She poured the dog food into the dog's bowl, then replaced the bag in the cupboard.

"*Casey.*"

She nearly slammed the cupboard door, her heart pounding at the whispered word. Mom and Chucky were talking and eating at the kitchen table. They hadn't called her, and they looked like they hadn't heard it either.

"*Casey.*"

Trembling, Casey looked out the kitchen window again. Althea was hovering near the gravel lane. She smiled softly, but her eyes were the same sad gray as before. As gray as the gathering dusk. As gray as the uniform of the man who had killed her in battle.

Chapter Nine

Proof from the Past

Casey was just finishing her chores at the stables when Zach came running in, waving a sheet of paper over his head.

"She wrote back! That lady wrote to us, Casey! Aunt Penny forwarded us the email she sent."

Casey whipped her gloves off and took the paper from Zach. "Did you read it already?"

"Not all of it. Come on, read it out loud."

They walked to the doorway where the sunlight hit the paper. Casey read the small print.

Dear Casey Coppersmith,

I'm sorry it took a couple of days to write back to you. I'm not at the Historical Society every day, so I waited and took your email along with me to work on Tuesday.

The first thing I checked was the census record of Carroll County, Maryland, for the year 1870. I found an eight-year-old boy named William Daniels living with Jennie and Charles Redding in Westminster at that time. If this is the boy, then these must have been his mother's parents. His grandmother was sixty-two years old at the time and his grandfather sixty-five. The record shows that they were running a local hardware store. There is a good chance that these people left behind a will that could tell us more. I have some Carroll County cemetery books at home and I will see if I can find a death date for any of them. Then, I will try to find a will.

That was all I could do Tuesday because I also have to help people who come into the Historical Society with their research. I will contact you again soon.

When did you meet up with Livy? She is right. I like a puzzle!

Sue Bundy

"She left her phone number, too," Casey said.

Zach grinned. "This is great! At least you can tell your ghost that her son stayed with her parents for good."

"Althea. Her name is Althea and she's not *my* ghost," Casey said. She looked thoughtful. "We don't know for sure if it's him though," she added.

Zach blew a breath of air up under his bangs. "Isn't it cool that you can find stuff like that? I bet you can find out about almost anyone, what with census records and cemetery records, and all the other records people kept. I didn't know about that. Did you?"

"Nope." Casey folded the paper neatly. "I wouldn't have known where to start." She slid the paper into her back pocket. "Did Philip see this?"

"Yeah. He printed it out for you and said he'd email thanks to Aunt Penny."

Casey walked slowly to the gate and let Zach and herself out. "There's something I don't understand about ghosts, Zach."

"What's that?"

Casey leaned back against the fence and squinted up at the sun. "Well, if ghosts can appear and disappear, and even get into your dreams, how come Althea doesn't *know* what happened to her son? Isn't he a ghost now, too? Why can't ghosts find each other?"

Zach wrinkled his nose as he thought. "I don't know. I think it's like Sam. Remember how we told you about him?"

"That little boy in the camper? Yeah, I remember," she said.

Zach was squinting up into the sky now. He blinked and looked back toward Casey. "One of Jared's friends went...well, wherever he went, and brought Sam's parents to the ghost ring, and to their son. Maybe some ghosts can't go anywhere."

"So maybe Althea is stuck here for good. She can't get to her husband or son?"

"Maybe she can't. Remember how Jared said it took a long time for Althea to learn to become solid, so we could see her?"

Casey nodded.

"Maybe it takes a long time to learn how to do other things too, like traveling, and finding your friends. Or maybe she doesn't need to see him, just wants to know how things went for her son."

Casey let out a growl of frustration. "There's too many maybes! Maybe this, and maybe that! *Maybe* she should have left this whole ghost business to you three boys!"

Casey turned on her heel and stomped off toward the store.

"Where are you going?" Zach called.

"I don't know. The pool, I guess."

Zach bit down on his bottom lip. He figured Casey was so steamed up she'd make a sizzle noise when she jumped in. He might have followed her to find out, but his stomach was growling with its own frustration. Hunger won out, and he ran off toward the snack bar.

"There you are," Mrs. Coppersmith said and sat a plate on the counter with a tuna salad sandwich and a bag of chips. Chucky and Philip were already eating.

"Did you find Casey?" Philip asked.

"Yeah. She said she was going to the pool."

Mrs. Coppersmith sighed. "That girl never eats when I want her to eat." She ripped a square of plastic wrap from the roll that hung over her worktable and began wrapping the extra tuna salad sandwich. "And she's supposed to take her dog for a walk. Chucky, if she doesn't come back by the time you're done, will you do it?"

Zach and Philip both smiled over their sandwiches. They knew how Chucky hated walking that little white poodle around on its shiny pink leash.

Chucky was about to say no, when his mom turned around with the wrapped sandwich in her hand and smiled, and he just couldn't. "I guess so, Mom."

Mrs. Coppersmith smiled even bigger. "Thanks."

Chucky elbowed Philip. "Take a walk with me?"

"We'll all walk her, Chucky," Zach answered for Philip. He didn't mind the poodle at all. Zach figured a dog is a dog.

After lunch, Chucky, Philip, and Zach headed out of the Coppersmith cottage with one happy little poodle.

"Let's go by the pool first," Chucky said, tugging on the brim of his Yankees cap. "If Casey is there, I want her to see I'm walking Prissy."

At the sound of her name, Prissy hesitated, and looked up at Chucky.

"Get moving," he said with a growl.

"She doesn't know where you want her to go," Philip said.

"Well, she won't stay beside me," Chucky complained. "Look at her prancing! She acts like she's leading a parade."

There wasn't any sign of Casey at the pool. Only a few campers were swimming.

As they walked, Zach told Philip and Chucky about Casey's reaction to the email. "And she's right, when you think about it," he said. "How come ghosts don't seem able to find each other unless they died near the same spot? Do they really get stuck where they died? How come you hear stories about ghosts haunting places they loved in life, or haunting cemeteries. They didn't die in the cemeteries where they are buried!"

Chucky veered off the gravel drive and onto a path that led deeper into the woods. He shivered. "I don't really want to know how it works," he said.

Philip laughed. "There are a lot of things we might never figure out about Jared, or any of the ghosts around here. But, we don't *have to* figure it out."

Zach snorted. "For people who don't have to figure out ghosts, we sure get involved in a lot of their problems."

Prissy liked walking in the woods. She ran from side to side, checking out all the ferns and other green growth along the path. She had the pink leash pulled tight.

"Don't let that big dog pull your arm out of its socket," Zach teased Chucky.

"Yeah, right," Chucky answered.

Then, Prissy stopped dead in her tracks. Her head came up straight and she stared down the path. The boys stopped too.

"What was that?" Philip whispered.

"It sounded like a growl," Zach said, staring at the little poodle with an amused expression.

"Yeah, right," Chucky said.

But then, Jared was there in front of the poodle. She yelped and danced backwards to get behind Chucky's legs.

"Hello, Corporal," Chucky said.

"I didn't mean to scare the little dog," Jared said.

"Casey wasn't around, so we had to walk her dog," Chucky explained.

"That was nice of you." Jared smiled. "I saw Casey a little while ago. She was sitting on the edge of the bridle path." Jared pointed to the left. "She looked sad."

"We found some information about Althea's son," Philip said. "At least we think it's him. But Casey's starting to wonder about things, the way ghosts work, I guess."

"She got all steamed up over nothing this morning," Zach said.

Prissy was jumping up and down behind Chucky. He finally turned and picked the dog up in his arms. Her white curls were soft and fluffy and her whole body trembled. "It's okay," he said quietly to her. "This is our friend, Corporal Scott."

Chucky took a step towards his ghost friend, and when Prissy growled he shushed her. "Don't growl at him. He's nice." He stepped even closer. Prissy pressed herself against Chucky and hid her face under his chin.

"Pet her once, Corporal."

"Maybe I shouldn't."

"I don't want her growling and shaking like a leaf every time you come around. She could give you away or something."

"All right, Chucky. I'll try." The corporal reached a hand toward Prissy. She pushed herself tighter against Chucky and shook, but this time she didn't growl.

"Hello, Prissy," Jared said softly. "You're a pretty girl, a good girl."

The poodle took her head from under Chucky's chin and looked at Jared's face. She blinked as his hand came near her again. But her shaking had stopped.

"Hey," Chucky said, "I think she's okay." He put her down and she sniffed at Jared's boots, then went back to the side of the path.

"See that, Chucky?" Philip asked. "It looks like Casey's got herself a ghost-detecting dog."

"Hey, she might be good to have around," Zach added.

Chucky wasn't impressed. "I'm glad she's good for something more than holding up her end of the leash," he said.

Philip and Zach laughed. They laughed even harder when the corporal said, "I wonder what she'd have to say about your end?"

* * * * *

Philip decided to check the email one more time before going to bed. He was glad he did. There was another forwarded message from Sue Bundy, sent by Aunt Penny. He read it to himself.

Dear Casey Coppersmith,

It is your boy. I found Charles Redding in a Westminster, Maryland, cemetery. He died October 12, 1880. So, this afternoon I went to the courthouse and found his will. He leaves money to his daughter, Eliza, and her children, and, it says, "to my grandson, William, son of my daughter Althea, who went off to soldier."

Knowing for sure it is the guy you wanted, I looked though the marriage books and found that he married a Lydia Cooper on February 14, 1882. There was a wedding announcement in the local paper. It says he was a lawyer, and there was a photo. I've scanned the photo and attached it below.

Both William and Lydia were buried at a Methodist cemetery in Carroll County. He died on June 8, 1924.

Lydia died on April 10, 1938. There is one infant child buried with them, born and died in 1886. I won't know of other children unless I go back to the courthouse and look for his will. Do you want me to do that?

Let me know—

Sue Bundy

There was the grainy black and white photo, attached at the end of the email. Philip stared at the couple in the picture. Neither one smiled, but they made an attractive couple. Maybe Casey could show Althea the photograph.

Philip printed out the email. He'd give it to Casey in the morning, so she could write a thank-you note to Sue Bundy, and decide what she would share with Althea.

As he shut down the computer he wondered what all this information would end up doing. Would Althea be happy with what they had discovered? How could it help her?

He thought it was awful nice of this Sue Bundy to do all this and not even know why. But then, would she even believe their story if she did?

Chapter Ten

Finding Peace

Casey stared at the black and white photo that Philip had printed from the computer. Althea's grown son stared out at her. He was young, tall and thin, with a mustache, and he was dressed in a dark suit, the jacket longer than most. His hand stretched out, holding the hand of Lydia, his new wife. Lydia was a pretty woman. She was wearing a Victorian style dress with lace on the arms and lace sweeping across the skirt at an angle. Although she couldn't tell its actual color in the black and white photo, Casey could tell that the dress was not white, like most of the wedding dresses she had seen. But the tiny white buttons that went up the front pulling the bodice tight, made the dress look fancy.

She had thought it impossible to find information about Althea's son, but Sue Bundy had done it, and she'd found a photograph, something Althea could see. Casey looked up at Philip, who had been waiting patiently for her reaction to the email.

"Sue Bundy found what you wanted, didn't she?" he said quietly.

"Even more." Casey suddenly felt like crying and she wasn't sure why.

Philip cleared his throat and jiggled the keys that hung from his belt. "I have to check the soda machines. Want to walk along? Maybe we'll run into Chucky, and we can show him the email, too."

"Sure." Casey shuffled the papers in her hand into a neat stack. "Did Zach already read it?"

"Yeah. I showed it to him last night." Philip laughed. "Good thing I did, 'cause you know Zach. He's still in bed. I wanted to find you first thing this morning, so you could read it for yourself, and decide what to do."

Casey fell into step beside Philip as he walked down the gravel camp road. "I'm glad you didn't tell me about the photo on the last page. It was good that I read the email first."

"Yeah."

"I still can't believe she did it." Casey folded the papers and put them in her back pocket. "That she found all this information, and so quickly, too."

"People who like to study genealogy, like this Sue Bundy, really get into it. Dad says they get obsessed and can't stop."

"I'm glad!" Casey said. "Hey, I bet that's why Livy said her aunt likes a mystery."

"Will you read the email to Althea? Will you show her the picture?"

Casey nodded. "Yes. I will do both. I just hope it's enough."

* * * * *

Jared led them up the hill to find Althea. Casey followed the crunch of his footsteps, even though she now knew the way by heart. As they walked, she thought about what she would say, replaying it in her mind again and again. "*Your son lived a fine life*, she would say. *He became a lawyer and married and...*would she mention the infant child? *No*, she answered herself. Some things were better left unsaid. Unless Althea asked. *Darn,* Casey thought. *I hope she doesn't ask.*

"Watch where you're going, Casey," Chucky grumbled as her foot crunched down on the back of his heel, skinning the sneaker from his foot.

"I'm sorry." Casey stopped and waited while Chucky slid his foot back into his sneaker. "I wasn't paying attention."

"No joke!" Chucky huffed.

"I can't stop thinking about Althea, and what I should tell her."

"Just tell her what Sue Bundy told you in the email," Philip suggested.

"What about the infant that died? Her grandchild? Should I tell her about that?"

Jared's deep voice startled Chucky. "Tell her whatever she asks," he said.

Zach stepped up next to Casey to tell her what Jared had said.

"That's what I thought, too," Casey said. Somehow she felt better, knowing that Jared had come to the same conclusion.

Philip had been leading them up the hill. Now at the top of the hill, he turned and walked toward the spot where Althea and Casey had met before. He stopped just short, putting his foot up on the log where he'd waited the last time. "We're here," he announced.

Jared gestured toward the clearing. "Althea is here, too," he said.

Casey didn't hear Jared. She didn't have to. She saw Althea. The ghost woman sat on a large outcropping of rock, her dress neatly spread around her legs, looking more solid than ever. Casey couldn't feel her feet moving as she walked to greet her.

"Jared tells me you have news of my son." Althea's face was creamy white, almost glowing. "I knew you would find news for me." She smiled at Casey.

All of the fear and apprehension Casey had bottled up inside drained away. Althea was her friend. She felt it stronger than she'd felt anything in years. She moved closer, to stand by Althea's knee.

Althea reached out and touched Casey's soft hair.

Casey felt static electricity pass through her and a soft breeze ruffled the curls that sprang from her ponytail.

"What do you have for me?"

Casey reached into her pocket and pulled out the folded note. "Your son lived with your parents until he was grown. He studied to become a lawyer, and he married."

Althea closed her eyes, her smile spreading as warm as the circle of light that was growing around her.

Casey unfolded the picture beneath the note, smoothing out the wrinkles. "This is a picture of your son with his wife, Lydia. You can see how happy they were."

Althea opened her eyes and stared at the picture. She reached out to take it, her long, slender fingers rustling the paper in Casey's hands.

Casey let go, but the paper dropped, fluttering down to the moss-covered earth below. "Oh," Casey grimaced, then leaned to pick up the paper. "Jared told me it took him a long time to learn how to pick things up, too," she said. She held the paper out again.

Althea shook her head, and Casey lowered her hand.

"I don't have to take it with me here," she said, stretching out her hand, palm up. "I can take it with me here." This time Althea put her palm across her chest, showing Casey that she would carry her son in her heart.

Althea looked down at the paper once more.

Casey smoothed it out again, so Althea could get a better look.

Althea stared, long and hard, then she nodded. "I will carry it with me always, where I have carried my infant son for years."

Casey nodded. "Will you ever find him? Will you ever see him again?"

"Perhaps..." Althea was fading. She had stayed solid longer than ever, but now her image was getting shaky.

"I'll carry someone else in my heart, too," she whispered softly. "Someone new from the land of the living." She smiled. "Casey, I will always carry you in my heart."

* * * * *

That night, after pinning the picture of William and Lydia on the bulletin board over her desk, Casey gazed out the bedroom window. Moonlight danced on a nylon tent pitched near the edge of the woods. Her brother, Chucky, and the Baxter boys were sleeping out. For once, Casey didn't feel left out. Her thoughts turned to the things Althea had taught her about war, mostly without ever knowing she had.

War is so sad, Casey thought. *It hurts the living, and it hurts the dead, and like a cannon's shot, it shakes the very foundation of family...and keeps doing it for years. It's only a whisper in the history texts, but it's a roar inside someone's heart.*

Casey rolled over. Her mind turned to what Althea said about carrying those she loved in her heart. *That's where Althea will stay,* Casey thought, touching her chest. She felt the gentle beat of her own heart and closed her eyes, remembering Althea.

* * * * *

Chucky rolled over in the tent. "What a summer of ghosts. Now, even Casey has one."

"Yeah, I had Sam for awhile," Zach said quietly. "But I know he's happy now."

"Aunt Penny had her soldier, too," Philip pitched in, then chuckled. "And that Byron Skelly had a whole pack of them breathing down his neck."

They all laughed, and Chucky said, "Gee, I wonder if it will ever end? Who will be next? Your dad?"

"Yikes," Zach squeaked. "Don't even think that!"

Philip zipped up his sleeping bag. "You can tell fall is coming. It's getting chilly."

"Who wants to dress as a ghost for Halloween this year?"

"Shut up, Chucky," Zach said, tossing a pillow at him.

Outside the tent, someone laughed. The boys turned toward the sound, and watched the blue glow leave their tent site, heading toward Ghost Ring Hill.

No one had to say a word. They were all thinking the same thing. No matter what, they had their ghost friend, and Corporal Jared Scott wasn't going anywhere.

THE END

Fact-finders

Look for books about ghosts or the Civil War in your school and public libraries. For more information on the Battle of Gettysburg and the supposed ghosts that haunt that area, here are two places for you to contact.

Gettysburg National Military Park
1195 Baltimore Pike
Gettysburg, Pennsylvania 17325
(717) 334-1124

Or visit the National Park Service on the web at www.nps.gov and follow the links to the park of your choice.

Ghosts of Gettysburg
271 Baltimore Street
Gettysburg, Pennsylvania 17325
(717) 337-0445
www.ghostsofgettysburg.com

Call or write to find out how to order Mark Nesbitt's books or take a ghost tour of Gettysburg. Tell Mr. Nesbitt the Gettysburg Ghost Gang sent you!

If you'd like to see a Gettysburg Ghost Gang Club formed, send a postcard with your name and address to:

Gettysburg Ghost Gang
P.O. Box 70
Arendtsville, Pennsylvania 17303

The Authors

SHELLEY SYKES has always been interested in ghosts and history. Living near the Gettysburg National Military Park gives her the opportunity to learn more about both. Her first young adult novel, *For Mike*, received an Edgar Allan Poe Award nomination for best young adult mystery and has been nominated for several state book awards. When not writing, Shelley Sykes is active in Girl Scouts and investigates ghosts and haunted locations.

LOIS SZYMANSKI is the author of 15 books for young readers, including *Little Icicle* and *Sea Feather*. She is the only author in the state of Maryland to start a writing club for children, under the umbrella of the 4-H program. She also created a program in which children can exhibit their writing at a county fair, and have it evaluated by professional writers from the community. Lois Szymanski has written for numerous children's publications, including *Highlights For Children* and *U*S*Kids Magazine*. She is regional advisor for the Maryland/Delaware/West Virginia sector of the Society of Children's Book Writers and Illustrators.

GETTYSBURG GHOST GANG

THE GHOST COMES OUT: *Gettysburg Ghost Gang #1*

The discovery of a ghost at the Gettysburg Battlefield is just the beginning of many adventures for three young friends.

978-1-57249-266-0 • PB

GHOST ON BOARD: *Gettysburg Ghost Gang #2*

Three young friends must rely on the help of their ghost-friend, Corporal Jared Scott, to solve the mystery of a new ghost that appears at the Cavalry Ridge Campground.

978-1-57249-267-7 • PB

NIGHTMARE: *Gettysburg Ghost Gang #3*

An eerie encounter with what turns out to be a ghost-horse sends the boys scrambling to their ghost-friend, Corporal Jared Scott, for help.

978-1-57249-268-4 • PB

GHOST HUNTER: *Gettysburg Ghost Gang #4*

Philip, Zach, and Chucky find themselves in a ghostly jam at Cavalry Ridge Campground when a ghost hunter arrives in Gettysburg.

978-1-57249-298-1 • PB

WHITE MANE PUBLISHING CO., INC.

To Request a Catalog Please Write to:

WHITE MANE PUBLISHING COMPANY, INC.
P.O. Box 708 • Shippensburg, PA 17257
e-mail: marketing@whitemane.com
Our catalog is also available online
www.whitemane.com

CPSIA information can be obtained
at www.ICGtesting.com
Printed in the USA
BVHW041950270920
589425BV00008B/63

9 781572 493278